THE U.S. MILITARY:
DEFENDING THE NATION

Lissette Gonzalez

PowerKiDS
press.
New York

Published in 2008 by The Rosen Publishing Group, Inc.
29 East 21st Street, New York, NY 10010

First Edition

Editor: Jennifer Way
Book Design: Greg Tucker
Photo Researcher: Nicole Pristash

Photo Credits: Cover © Tyler Stableford/Getty Images; p. 5 by Helene C. Stikkel/Dept. of Defense; p. 7 © Dept. of Defense; pp. 9, 11 © Shutterstock.com; p. 13 © Bullit Marquez/AFP/Getty Images; p. 15 © U.S. Navy/Getty Images; p. 17 by Senior Airman Sean Sides/Dept. of Defense; p. 19 © Petty Officer 2nd Class Luke Pinneo/U.S. Coast Guard via Getty Images; p. 21 © Ahmad Al-Rubaye/AFP/Getty Images.

Library of Congress Cataloging-in-Publication Data

Gonzalez, Lissette.
   The U.S. military : defending the nation / Lissette Gonzalez.
      p. cm. — (Dangerous jobs)
   Includes index.
   ISBN-13: 978-1-4042-3777-3 (library binding)
   ISBN-10: 1-4042-3777-1 (library binding)
   1. United States—Armed Forces—Juvenile literature. 2. Soldiers—United States—Juvenile literature.
   3. National security—United States—Juvenile literature. I. Title.
   UA23.G72567 2008
   355.00973—dc22

                                             2006038401

Manufactured in the United States of America

CONTENTS

THE U.S. MILITARY

People who work in the U.S. military defend the country and its people. The military has five branches. They are the Army, the Navy, the Marine Corps, the Air Force, and the Coast Guard.

Each military branch has a different specialty. The Army **protects** the country on land. The Navy protects the country at sea. The Air Force uses aircraft to defend the country. The Marine Corps quickly brings military force into troubled places. The Coast Guard protects the country's coasts, ports, and waterways. Each branch faces many dangers. This book will teach you what military **careers** are like.

These U.S. Army soldiers are wearing their dress uniforms. Dress uniforms are the clothes worn on special occasions. Each military branch has different styles of dress uniform and combat uniform.

BOOT CAMP

The first step in joining any military branch is to go to that branch's boot camp. In boot camp **recruits** do **physical** exercise **routines** every day to get into shape. Recruits also learn to use and take care of **weapons**, such as guns. They also learn how to operate military **vehicles**, such as aircraft, jeeps, or boats.

Boot camp also gets recruits' minds ready for **combat**. Recruits learn how to follow orders from their leaders and to work as a team. Teamwork is important in the military because troops in combat need to work together to stay alive.

These Air Force recruits are learning combat exercises in boot camp.

7

MILITARY GEAR AND VEHICLES

Troops in combat wear clothes called body armor. Body armor helps protect them from enemy fire. Body armor is lined with strong, yet lightweight, stuff called Kevlar. Kevlar is so strong that it can stop **bullets** from AK-47 guns from killing the person wearing it!

Protective clothing is not the only advanced gear used by people in the military. Soldiers may wear glasses that allow them to see at night. They may drive special combat vehicles, such as the Stryker. Some troops fly fighter planes, such as the F-16. Others might learn to operate ships or fly helicopters.

The F-16 is used by the U.S. Air Force. This fighter plane is also known as the Fighting Falcon. A falcon is a bird known for its strength.

9

THE U.S. ARMY

People who serve in the Army are called soldiers. Soldiers put their skills to use in different **units** of the Army.

In **infantry** units soldiers fight on foot. They use guns and other small weapons. The U.S. Army uses the infantry to fight on land.

The infantry works with the **artillery** units. Artillery units fire bombs and shells at an enemy.

Some soldiers serve in the Army's Special Forces unit, known as the Green Berets. Green Berets often take part in very dangerous **missions**, sometimes in enemy territory.

10

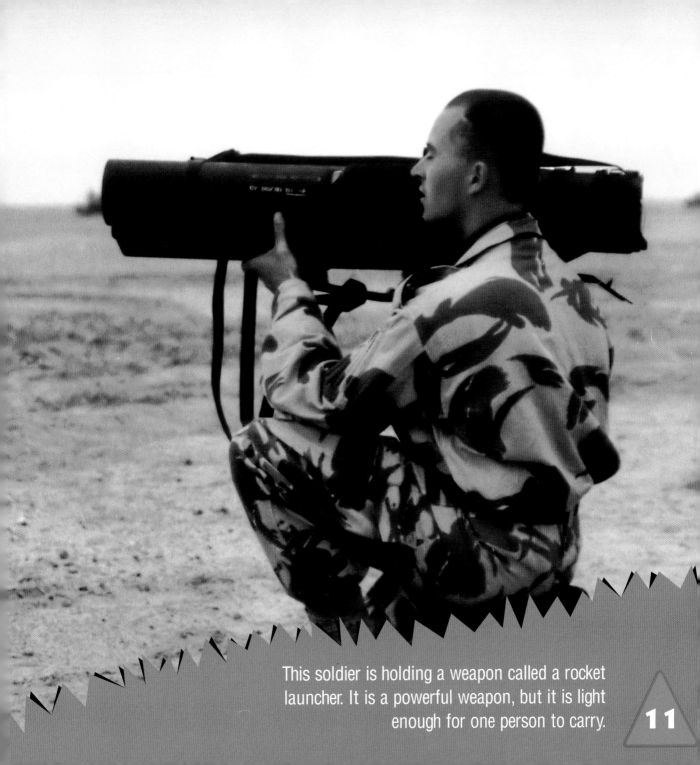

This soldier is holding a weapon called a rocket launcher. It is a powerful weapon, but it is light enough for one person to carry.

THE U.S. MARINE CORPS

The Marine Corps is considered one of the hardest military jobs. Marine Corps training camps are famous for being hard to finish.

The Marine Corps is really a part of the U.S. Navy that **specializes** in amphibious warfare. "Amphibious" means that something is both in water and on land. The Marine Corps uses the Navy to move its people, weapons, and aircraft.

Marines are often the first U.S. troops to arrive in troubled places. They come in from the sea and try to clear the way on land for other soldiers.

These Marines are practicing an amphibious attack. In this kind of attack, they go from the water to land without having to stop fighting.

13

THE U.S. NAVY

People who serve in the U.S. Navy are called sailors. About 375,000 sailors have active-duty jobs. Being on active duty means working full-time in the military. Sailors on active duty work in naval bases or on ships all over the world.

Aircraft carriers are the Navy's largest, most powerful ships. They carry airplanes and helicopters that can take off from the carriers at sea. Thousands of sailors are needed to operate an aircraft carrier.

Navy SEALs are the Navy's special forces unit. Navy SEALs go through hard training that prepares them for dangerous missions.

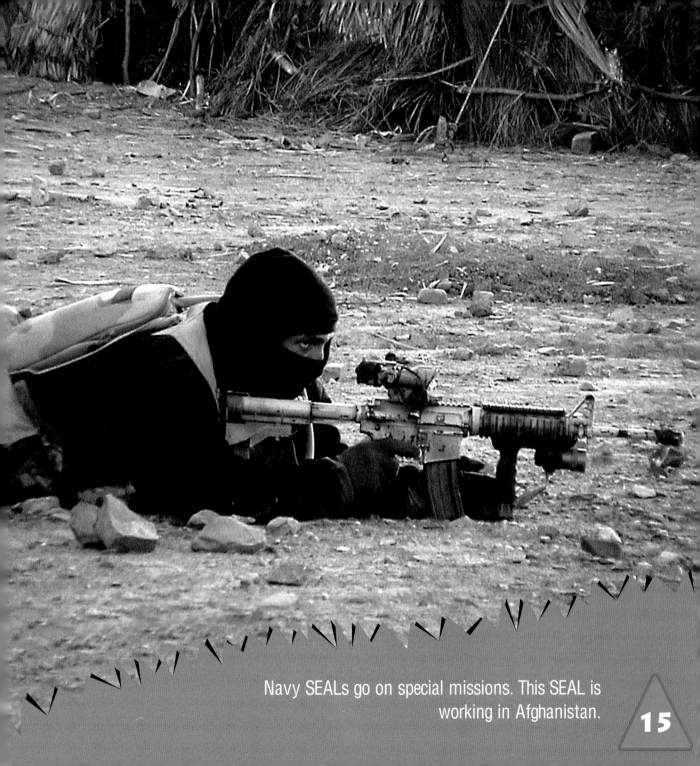

Navy SEALs go on special missions. This SEAL is
working in Afghanistan.

THE U.S. AIR FORCE

Although most of its troops work on the ground, the U.S. Air Force is famous for its fighter planes and the pilots who fly them. Fighter planes are very fast. Most are used to fight other aircraft. Some, like the F-22 Raptor, can also hit objects on the ground.

Not all pilots fly in combat. Test pilots have one of the most dangerous jobs in the Air Force. Test pilots fly new airplanes or fly in ways that have never been tried before. Then they can tell the Air Force whether a new plane or a flight move is safe. Test pilots work at the U.S. Air Force Flight Test School, at Edwards Air Force Base, in California.

Air Force fighter pilots learn to fly many types of planes. This airman is flying an F-16.

17

THE U.S. COAST GUARD

The Army, Navy, Marine Corps, and Air Force are part of the U.S. Department of Defense. The Coast Guard is a little different. During wartime the Coast Guard is part of the Department of Defense, like the other branches. However, during peacetime the Coast Guard operates as part of the Department of Homeland Security.

The Coast Guard has an important part in keeping the country safe. Its saying is "Always ready." People who work in the Coast Guard look after port, coast, and waterways security at home so the Navy can do its work all over the world.

18

The Coast Guard defends the nation's ports. This Coast Guard boat is patrolling the harbor in Boston, Massachusetts.

GOING TO WAR

Countries may go to war for different reasons. Countries have gone to war over things such as territory and beliefs.

People who join the military know that at some point they may be called upon to fight in a war. This is the most dangerous part of a career in the military. Troops know that they may be hurt or even killed as they perform their duties. Going to war has killed hundreds of thousands of American troops over the United States' 231-year history. A great number have been hurt on active duty and lived.

These U.S. Army troops have been sent
to fight in Iraq.

REWARDS OF A MILITARY CAREER

Even though they have some of the most dangerous jobs around, people in the military often say that they love what they do. War may be scary, but troops know that part of their job is also to help people and serve their country.

Above all, members of the U.S. military have the satisfaction of knowing that they defend and protect their country. The hardest jobs can turn out to be the most **rewarding**.

GLOSSARY

artillery (ahr-TIH-lur-ee) The part of an army that uses large guns, such as cannons.

bullets (BU-lets) Things that are shot out of a gun.

careers (kuh-REERZ) Jobs.

combat (KOM-bat) A battle or a fight.

infantry (IN-fun-tree) The part of an army that fights on foot.

missions (MIH-shunz) Special jobs.

physical (FIH-zih-kul) Having to do with the body.

protects (pruh-TEKTS) Keeps safe.

recruits (rih-KROOTS) New members of a group.

rewarding (rih-WOR-ding) Feeling good about something you have done.

routines (roo-TEENZ) Doing something the same way over and over.

specializes (SPEH-shuh-lyz-ez) Does something very well.

units (YOO-nets) Groups of soldiers.

vehicles (VEE-uh-kulz) Means of moving or carrying things.

weapons (WEH-punz) Tools used by troops, such as guns or bombs.

INDEX

WEB SITES

Due to the changing nature of Internet links, PowerKids Press has developed an online list of Web sites related to the subject of this book. This site is updated regularly. Please use this link to access the list:
www.powerkidslinks.com/djob/usmil/

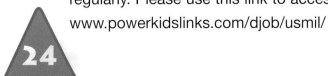
24